In memory of my father, Lt. j.g. Zack David Holland.
His proudest memories were of serving his country at sea during World War II.
—*T.H.*

Lt. Brian Musfeldt, USS *Abraham Lincoln*, CVN72:
Thank you for your service and for your help with this book. —*C.F. and T.H.*

Text copyright © 2014 by Trish Holland and Christine Ford
Illustrations copyright © 2014 by John Manders
All rights reserved.
Published in the United States by Golden Books, an imprint of Random House Children's Books, a division of Random House LLC, 1745 Broadway, New York, NY 10019. Golden Books, A Golden Book, and the G colophon are registered trademarks of Random House LLC.
Visit us on the Web!
randomhouse.com/kids
Educators and librarians, for a variety of teaching tools, visit us at RHTeachersLibrarians.com
Library of Congress Control Number: 2012952463
ISBN 978-0-385-36998-5 (trade) — ISBN 978-0-375-97180-8 (lib. bdg.)
MANUFACTURED IN CHINA
10 9 8 7 6 5 4 3 2 1

The Navy's Night Before Christmas

By Trish Holland and Christine Ford

Illustrated by John Manders

🌼 A GOLDEN BOOK · NEW YORK

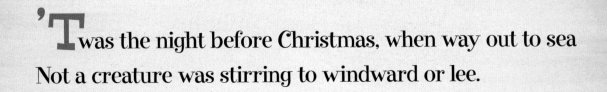

'Twas the night before Christmas, when way out to sea
Not a creature was stirring to windward or lee.

The sailors were nestled all snug in their racks
Like orders of pancakes, so tight were the stacks.
All dreamed of home port and Christmases past
Among family and friends—sweet memories that last.

And I, in the tower, had just reached my post,
Where I'd stand the watch. It was Christmas—almost!

My thoughts about presents were shattered by sound.
A WHUMP-WHUMP-WHUMP-WHUMP had me
  spinning around.
I looked to the starboard, then port, bow, and aft.
The noise, it grew louder. I felt a cold draft.

When, what to my wondering eyes should appear
But a Seahawk that hovered. I gave the all clear.

A squadron of Hornets—
so loudly they roared!—
With tailhooks a-hangin'
came blasting aboard.

The sonar went crazy!
A sub was about.
It popped to the surface
with SEALs pouring out.

A deafening drone froze me fast to the floor.
A Greyhound then stopped and threw open its door,
And down jumped a sailor as carols came blaring.
It was Master Chief Claus! I just couldn't stop staring.

A salty old dog, he was all chest and arm.
I bet he could bench-press a Jeep with no harm.
The man was clean-shaved, with a block for a chin.
His eyes could bore holes to the back of your skin.

He paced on the flight deck; then quickly he spun.
He mustered his crew, called their names one by one:
"Garcia and Washington, Collins and Yee,
and Williams and Rubin, and Clark and Ali.

"Our mission tonight: to take care of our own,
Bringing joy to our sailors with gifts straight from home.
You each know your jobs, so I will be brief.
Work quickly, you swabbies!"

"Aye-aye, Master Chief!"

"Go fill up my seabags with gifts large and small.
Now dash away, dash away, dash away, all!"

He shouldered his pack and he twisted the latch.
Then the Chief disappeared through a big metal hatch.

I raced down to find him, with no time to spare.
I checked by my rack, 'cause I knew he'd stop there.

And right by the tree stood a glorious sight—
Our Master Chief Claus spreading Christmas delight.
The bunks were all covered with goodies galore,
With cookies and pictures and presents from shore.

And on each sailor's bed, both below and above,
Lay a quilt made at home, every stitch set with love.

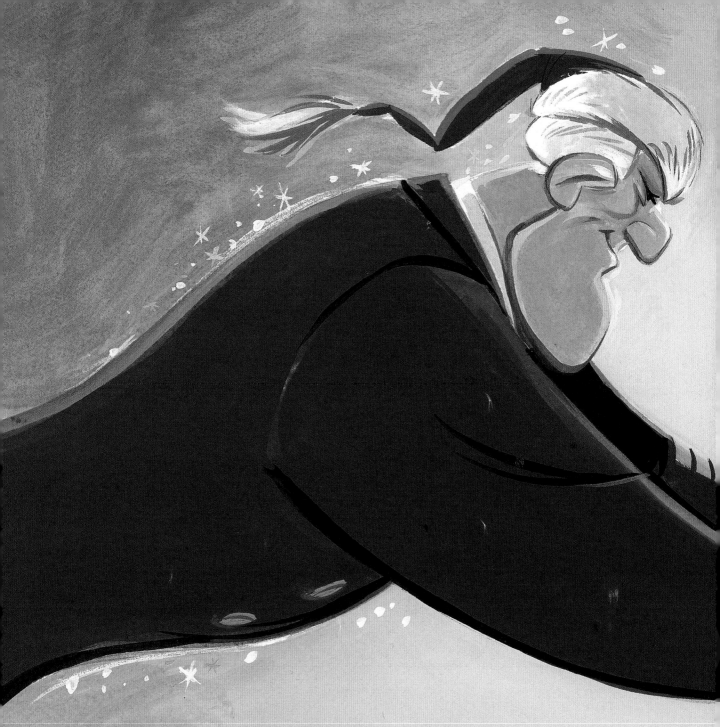

Claus gave me a look that was solemn and bold,
And he tacked on my chest, in tradition of old,
A medal for service above and beyond.
Yes, we are the Navy. We share a proud bond.

He lifted his hand with a movement so swift.
He snapped a salute as his last Christmas gift.
He was gone in an instant—I didn't know where—
But I heard rumbling engines preparing for air.

I rushed to the flight deck. The Hornets were screaming.
I saw Santa wave—and his face, it was beaming.

"Ho, ho, ho!" he exclaimed with a nod to his crew.
They shot to the stars. Away the planes flew!

As the ship's radar lost him came one final call—

"HAPPY CHRISTMAS,
BRAVE SAILORS!
MAY PEACE COME TO ALL!"